Bozwell
The Big
Red Dog

A story that will amuse the children that read it and
the adults that read it to them or for themselves.

A reminder of the trials and tribulations of family life.

Bozwell The Big Red Dog

Spiderwize
Remus House
Coltsfoot Drive
Woodston
Peterborough
PE2 9BF

www.spiderwize.com

A CIP catalogue record for this book is available from the British Library.

ISBN: 978-1-912694-61-7

BOZWELL THE BIG RED DOG

PHILIP ETHERTON

SPIDERWIZE
Peterborough UK
2018

Thank you Luke and Megan Huggins for helping me to write this book.

CONTENTS

CHAPTER 1

The Huggetts

All the puppies were excited, but one had Christmas Eve in his eyes. They met the Huggetts with a warm and trusting stare. The small Irish Setter puppy immediately showed the world that he was different from the rest by sitting at the entrance to the large kennel where the puppies lived.

Refusing to move, his brothers and sisters dashed around wildly jumping up in waves at the fence which separated them from the smiling faces behind it. These were the new prospective owners trying to identify the individual puppies which were to be the new addition to their families.

The dogs were no ordinary Irish Setters, but the Rochester breed which were recognisable by the distinctive white marking on their chest. At the moment is was only a "white flash" but it would, as they grew older, be worn proudly like a row of medals.

The Huggett's dog, who still remained firmly sat at the kennel entrance, was the grandson of Rochester Gentleman, who had won a prize as the supreme champion of Crufts a few years ago. Bozwell, as he was to be later called, seemed to know this as children draw strength from their parents and share many common characteristics.

Mr. Huggett, a tall, slim talkative man was joined at the fence by Mrs. Huggett, just as tall and slim but of a quieter nature. "Darling, he looks very small," remarked Mrs. Huggett. "Look at his paws," replied Mr. Huggett. "You can always tell how big a dog would be by the size of his paws."

Bozwell was indeed a small frame supported by four spindly pillars, one at each corner, rather like a new born deer. Mr and Mrs Huggett knew what he would look like when fully grown as they had obtained many books from the library on the subject of dogs and from hours of laborious reading and endless comparisons of other breeds, had selected an Irish Setter as being the type that would suit the Huggett family.

The main reason being they had two small children. The Irish Setter breed was noted for its gentleness.

It is indeed strange that although pedigree animals such as cats and dogs develop individually, their main character can be almost guaranteed by means of selective breeding.

There are some people that think that children should be produced in this way, but I don't think so. It is much more exciting to be surprised. When it comes to dogs however, it is useful to know in advance that they can swim, run, bark etc. It would be very strange to buy a greyhound that could not run, or a gun dog who could not smell or swim.

Mr. Huggett turned around for a moment and saw advancing towards him a large figure who appeared to be wearing a bright golden halo. It was caused by the sun which was setting behind him, as it was now becoming quite late. As he came closer and could be seen more clearly, Mr and Mrs Huggett guessed that this must be the owner of the kennels who bred and showed the Setters.

He had the type of weather beaten appearance that you would imagine farmers would have and obviously spent a great deal of time out of doors. His face opened up into a large smile, as he extended his hand to greet Mr and Mrs Huggett. "I'm Mr. Jones," he said. "We have spoken several times on the telephone." Indeed they had.

It was not a question of just selling a pet, Mr. Jones was very careful who he would let own and take care of his puppies. Several long conversations had taken place

before he had agreed that Mr and Mrs Huggett could be potential owners.

Meanwhile, Bozwell decided to vacate the entrance to the kennel, not without a little encouragement from Mrs. Huggett who had decided to coax him by hitting her knees with her hands and calling him to her. It was difficult to know what Bozwell made of this other than to decide it was worthy of investigation. He started towards the fence, slowly at first, then a trot, then a run, until a few metres from the fence he sprung into the air as if he wished to jump onto Mrs. Huggett's lap. From the corner of his eye, Mr. Huggett saw this and wondered if it was his imagination or did Bozwell appear to have jumped twice as high as the other puppies.

Mrs. Huggett stepped back in alarm as the red bundle thundered into the fence. Frightened that he would hurt himself she appeared anxious, but her fears were dissolved by Mr. Jones who assured her that they were very tough dogs and very strong. A fact that would become obvious to them later on.

Bozwell made a vain attempt to lick Mrs Huggett's hand, only succeeding in wedging his nose and mouth in the opening of the fence. With a small squeal he withdrew.

Not to be defeated however, he decided to attempt once again to jump over the two metre high fence. Mr. Huggett watched again in amazement as Bozwell sprang in the air performing a perfect somersault that a gymnast would have been proud of. "I think we had better go in doors, your puppy appears to be becoming too excited." said Mr. Jones.

They all entered the cosy living room of the house next to the kennel. The paper on the wall was hardly visible as it was covered with rosettes won at shows by the Rochester Setters over many years. The shelves on the mantelpiece were full of cups and shields won in similar fashion.

In every room there is one corner which is the focus of attention. Your eyes are automatically drawn to it by an invisible magnetism. It is unfortunately normally where the television is situated. This room was different. Instead of the television, it was a large comfortable chair, well- padded to afford its occupant every creature comfort. Indeed the creature in it was obviously enjoying every comfort.

The Irish Setter sat upright in the chair, as would a king surveying his court. Not exactly looking down on his subjects but aware that they are, in some small way, inferior to him. This dog had such a look and bearing that Mr and Mrs Huggett felt unsure as to whether or not they should nod their heads in respect, but limited their response to an incredulous smile. Bozwell, now asleep after his exertion, was blissfully unaware that his owners had just been introduced to his Grandfather.

Mr. Jones ushered the Huggetts into the centre of the room and offered them the second most comfortable seat, the settee, he being content to sit in an upright chair. While his wife was organising a pot of tea, Mr Huggett took the opportunity to study Rochester Gentleman at close quarters. He, the dog that is, had turned his head to look at them. A small movement of his tail indicated that he had acknowledged their presence, but was not interested enough to vacate his chair.

He was quite clearly advanced in years, even old. The brown eyes, however, had refused to surrender to Father Time and sparkled; it seemed to have a depth which reflected the quietness which arrives with age. They appeared to say "Yes I have done that, been there, found most of it boring, but I'm pleased I did it." The once red hair around his nose had taken the pleasure of autumn and was not quite as red as it once was; we would call it distinguished.

The tea arrived and Mr Huggett's attention was once again drawn to his host. There then began a most subtle interrogation which basically aimed at establishing whether or not Mr and Mrs Huggett would make suitable owners for Bozwell.

Rochester Gentleman appeared to be listening intently, as a judge who would deliberate eventually on whether or not the new owners would be allowed to take charge of his Grandson. "What type of house do you live in?" asked Mr. Jones. Mr. Huggett who took to automatically answering questions, an unfortunate habit, stated that the house, although a modest semi-detached, backed on to farmland which would allow a large dog, which eventually Bozwell would be, plenty of scope to exercise. Little did Mr Huggett realise that most of Bozwell's exercise would be spent without the benefit of his supervision!

The small fence which separated the modest garden from the enticing countryside would provide little discouragement for a dog who was sufficiently energetic at six weeks old to recently attack a two metre high fence.

This, however, was in the future and Mr Huggett was blissfully unaware of any potential problems.

Mr. Jones continued the line of questioning: "Children?" he asked. Mrs. Huggett intervened at this stage, possibly to prevent her husband from saying anything derogatory concerning their daughters Zoë and Michelle. "They are aged six and seven and a half and will delight in Bozwell."

She explained that as parents they were keen for the girls to be comfortable with pets and that she was sure that they would enjoy each other's company. For a moment Mr Huggett wondered whether it was fair or not to inflict his daughters on Bozwell. Whilst they could not be described as being really bad, they were very active and seemed to have almost as much energy as the little Irish Setter puppy.

Nevertheless, he was sure that Bozwell would be strong enough to look after himself and more than a match for the girls

As explained earlier, it was partly due to their robust behaviour that they had been careful in the selection of a breed. Mr. Jones on his behalf accepted that Mr and Mrs Huggett would be suitable owners and warned them that Irish Setters were not the easiest of animals in the world to own.

After the girls, thought Mr Huggett, anything else would be child's play. They shook hands, money exchanged during the process and from that moment they became the proud owners of Bozwell the Big Red Dog.

CHAPTER 2

Double Trouble

"Well!" (not a good way to start a sentence, but that's how Bozwell started his second day in the Huggett household.) "Well" he thought, "What now?" He had laid all night in the new wicker basket bought for him and, although the soft blanket under him was comfortable, it was not home.

In half expectation of suddenly being transported back to familiar places, he raised his small black nose above the basket and sniffed. Although his sense of smell was hundreds of times more powerful than his owners' he still could not smell the fresh hay that he had so recently left behind nor feel the presence of his brothers and sisters. He suddenly missed his mother and didn't feel like the strong lion of yesterday when excitement had momentarily numbed his brain. A small tear managed to squeeze its way past his eye and down his cheek, where it paused for a moment on his whiskers before being absorbed by the blanket.

Being alone can be a pleasant change from the noise of the playground, but if you feel particularly sad or worried about something, spirits can sink and you can start to feel sorry for yourself. Company can be the light that melts the gloom.

The light came in the shape of the girls. Having been expressly told by their parents not to disturb the dog, they quietly jumped up at the door handle and managed to fall through the door in a jumbled heap of nightgown and slippers. "Now we're in trouble", said Zoë and they both immediately resolved to blame each other for not doing what they had been told (this being a favourite trick to confuse their parents). Their introduction to Bozwell could not have been more comical and was one of those moments when you wished you had not broken the camera that Uncle Roger bought you for your birthday.

Dogs, like humans, often work purely on instinct. Can you remember doing something recently on impulse and thinking afterwards, "Why did I do that?" For a moment it feels as though your head has been switched off and somebody else is in control. Bozwell instinctively knew that the two bundles on the floor were friendly and were of no danger to him. So, he did what comes naturally to an excitable Irish Setter puppy. He jumped up out of his basket and landed on top of the bundle and started to lick furiously the space beneath the auburn fringe that belonged to Zoë, smothering her face with a thousand kisses, like some newly reunited lover. She squealed with delight and appeared to begin a wrestling match attempting to remove Bozwell, who had immediately forgotten about his past home and was thoroughly enjoying the game.

Underneath the heap, Zoë struggled to become free and in doing so knocked over the bowl of milk that had been put down for Bozwell the previous evening.

Up went the bowl, down came the milk. The game stopped instantly.The three of them sat on the floor looking at each other. Not for the last time were the three of them to be in trouble. The good thing about being a puppy or a young baby is that you do not know when you have done something wrong or are likely to be told off. Bozwell was in this peaceful state, but the girls were not! Although most of the milk had found its way onto tomorrow's washing, in the form of the girls' nightdresses, some of it had been deposited onto Bozwell. When Mrs Huggett had put the milk down for her new puppy's use, this was not quite what she had in mind. They sat in a circle, the stillness only being disturbed by the bowl settling into a stationary position, not at present being able to make up its mind where to stop as it rocked back and forth. Bozwell's tail was busy spreading the remainder of the milk over the floor, as it wagged back and forward with relentless energy. "What a splendid game!" he thought.

His boyish good looks had been momentarily changed into comical fashion by the milk deposited on his face. His eyes and nose were now contrasted by large white rings and the white flash on his chest matched by the one on the top of his head.

Although the girls were tempted to laugh, they heard the footsteps approaching downstairs. They knew this meant trouble, but Bozwell had yet to find out! Mr Huggett appeared first through the door and observed the freshly painted picture.

Mrs Huggett stood slightly behind him and nervously peered over his shoulder. In a raised voice, he gave the girls what can only be described as a severe telling off. It is always essential that mums and dads help each other raise their family, but many times they have different views on what is the best method of doing so. Mr Huggett believed in a disciplined approach, Mrs Huggett believed in a softer approach; she believed that they were not really naughty, just that they were accident prone. From the girls' point of view it really wasn't their fault most of the time when things happened.For the rest of the time, they were only guilty of forgetting what instructions they had been given, such as not to disturb the dog.

Their father's raised voice reminded them that their memories had let them down yet again, but they hoped by putting on their best and cutest look, that would be the end of the matter. In fact, Mrs Huggett was trying to hide a smile that had just been born on her lips and threatened to grow from ear to ear.

Mr Huggett afterwards had to admit that the girls and their playmate did look funny and it didn't take Mr Huggett long to clean up the mess left by their first game.

The girls were quickly spirited into a bath, where they proceeded once again to soak the bathroom carpet and Bozwell's hair was soon washed and dried. He had been startled by Mr Huggett's raised voice, being the first time he had heard it. Something inside of him recognised that he preferred the soft and normal way of communication. Harsh words were to be avoided.

He was let out into the garden and stretched his legs on the newly discovered freedom of Mr and Mrs Huggett's lawn. "Now this is more like it", he thought. As you will recall, the house backed onto farmland and open countryside.

The early morning breeze piped its call to Bozwell, explaining that beyond the fence there were adventures and fellow animals that were going about their daily business. Bozwell rushed around the garden, as if the gyroscope in his head were on holiday. Going in no particular direction he ran from one side of the garden to the other and then finding himself crashing into the flower beds, breaking three dahlias that had been quietly minding their own business while basking in the morning sun. Everything in life is relative.

You may think you are poor when your pocket money is all spent. In other parts of the world, they do not possess any pockets in the first place. So it was with Bozwell. Being only at the moment tiny, the flower border was a jungle adventure playground. Looking down he could see beetles and other small insects which inhabited the soil beneath the flowers. To them of course, he was a giant who could crush them with one light blow of his paws. Being of a gentle nature, this was the farthest thought from his mind and he contented himself with pushing them with his nose to investigate them. Having discovered that they did not smell good enough to eat, nor did they apparently want to play, he made an exit out of the jungle back onto the lawn.

The only evidence of his expedition was the soil that had been deposited on his nose. Once again he looked comical! Had his maker made a mistake with this creature? Should he have been born human and be destined to join a circus as a clown?

We will never know. He next decided to roll on his back, a favourite pastime of dogs, especially just after they have been given a bath. It may be that they have an itch; it may be that they wish to transfer the smell of the soil onto them for disguise. The ritual probably goes back thousands of years and I suspect they do not know why themselves, Bozwell just knew that he enjoyed it. His four legs thrashed about in the air rhythmically, the equivalent I guess of the 'Doggie Waltz', swaying left to right, right to left, they had the effect of moving his back in a circular motion on the lawn. He looked up to the sun and slowly revolved around, using his tail as a rudder. Could anything be more pleasant? Something wasn't quite right however, it smelt good, but not as good as it could be. Bozwell's nose was like radar.

He could smell the earth beneath the grass. It smelt soft and warm and how can it best be described? Just 'earthy.' He stopped dancing for a moment and decided to reach the treasure he knew was temptingly close. His mum had not needed to teach him to dig in order to bury bones for future use, just as you did not need showing how to eat when you were born. So with great efficiency, a small hole appeared in the lawn; earth showering from beneath his rear legs with his front paws tearing at the carefully tended grass. In no time Bozwell had removed his head from the hole and was once again on his back, but this time in the middle of a freshly dug pile of soil.

All this was being observed from the bedroom window by the two little towelled bundles who noticed the devastation on the lawn. Having previously performed a similar operation by pretending they were building sandcastles on the beach, they knew what the outcome would be. Michelle, the quiet thoughtful one of the two, turned to her sister and said "Daddy will be pleased".

CHAPTER 3

The Big Wide World

Have you ever thought that your world is as big or as little as you think it is or wish to make it? To a goldfish it is the size of a small bowl, a pond or if fortunate enough to be swimming in a lake. It was the same for Bozwell.

The first few months of his life was spent in the garden, which was modest in size and rapidly shrinking as he grew bigger. He could see the inviting lands beyond the fence, but so far had not plucked up the courage to attempt to break out of his exercise yard.

He was not aware that things were due to change and the cage door would soon be opened. Zoë and Michelle had accompanied Mr and Mrs Huggett into the small town of Dorrington, which was some four miles from where they lived. The girls did not particularly like shopping, nor did their parents particularly like taking them, but they certainly could not be left unsupervised at home. They stood in the pet shop looking at a selection of collars and leads for Bozwell. Mrs Huggett, although attentively listening to her husband's comments as to the size of the collar and the length of lead they should purchase, had a small part of her monitoring the girls.

It is well known fact that mothers have an invisible pair of eyes in the back of their head.

The last visit to a china shop had been quite expensive!

They had to pay for the jug Michelle had somehow managed to dislodge while attempting to wrap her pigtails round her neck by rapidly moving her head back and forth. They had never managed to obtain a satisfactory answer as to why she was attempting this particular exercise, however, accidents will happen.

This time the girls were pre-occupied by studying the animals, during which time a number of "please, please can we have one?" were directed at their parents.

The objects of their attention ranged from a loveable hamster to perhaps a not so loveable large spider that, believe it or not, some people keep as pets. Mrs Huggett, without a fuss, gently pulled Zoë's hand away from the parrot cage they were standing next to as she was about to attempt to stir the bird into action by prodding it with her finger, which was just small enough to pass between the bars. They left the shop without a mishap. The shiny collar and lead, smelling wonderfully of new leather, was held tightly by Zoë who was given the responsibility of carrying it home. Michelle had to be pacified by being given a packet of dog biscuits to carry, as the girls always insisted that there should never be any favouritism shown by their parents to their other half. As the car drew up on to the path, Mrs Huggett questioned her husband as to whether or not it was difficult to train dogs to walk on a lead.

Mr Huggett replied with all the authority of one who had never tried before: "I don't see any problems, dogs always look quite happy on a lead".

He was later to realise that this was not always the case. Bozwell had spent the morning scampering around the kitchen, playing with the toys that had been bought for his amusement. The rubber bone with bells inside was his favourite and he enjoyed tossing it in the air and attempting to catch it. Isn't it strange that no matter how much you wish for a particular toy, two days after Christmas life becomes boring again? It was exactly the same for Bozwell. He returned to his basket that was positioned thoughtfully under the radiator and pondered on what to do next.

The large basket had been purchased with a view to ensuring that it would be comfortable for him when he was fully grown, so at the moment when he sat in the middle of it, he looked rather like a cherry on top of an iced bun.

He moved closer to the edge of the basket to investigate its construction. It was not a modern plastic one, but an old-fashioned wicker basket with the strands at the side weaving in and out like waves. The top of the basket was neatly finished off with a clever pattern and this at the moment was receiving Bozwell's attention. His small needle- like teeth were beginning to nibble the top. By sitting upright and bracing himself with his front paws, he started to pull at the wicker.

To his delight the pattern began to unravel itself and he was able to chew the dislodged strands. He was not really being naughty and destructive. You probably cannot remember, but when your teeth are being born out of your gums, it is very comforting to be able to chew on something. It was so with Bozwell. The large back teeth, which would eventually be capable of crushing a large marrowbone, were now just starting to sprout; the chewing action was not only keeping him amused, but massaging this area of his mouth, which was extremely itchy.

I don't suppose the basket appreciated the service it was being given as one strand after another gave up its position in the pattern and surrendered itself to Bozwell's jaws. Some hours later, Bozwell certainly did not recognise the look of dismay on the faces of Mr and Mrs Huggett when they entered the kitchen. Zoë had been in the kitchen for some time and was busy wrestling with Bozwell the blue rubber ring being the only thing separating them at this moment, one half in Bozwell's mouth, and the other half in hers. Both trying, with a shake of the head, to gain total possession of the ring. "I told you not to do that" said Mr Huggett. "He might accidentally nip you, and it is also not very hygienic!" Zoë continued the game as she was confident that Bozwell would not be so careless as to nip her.

As she had not yet learnt the meaning of the word 'hygienic' and with her mouth preoccupied, she was not in a position to ask. She felt perfectly justified in ignoring her father on the grounds that she thought he was wrong.

It also served him right for using words she did not understand. A strong hand removed the ring from the battling couple which prematurely ended the game, much to both Zoë's and Bozwell's annoyance. Why do parents never have any fun? Bozwell changed his attention to Mr and Mrs Huggett wagging his tail furiously while they studied the basket.

Mr Huggett carried out a rapid temporary repair by binding the basket with tape, which Bozwell decided could wait until he had time to remove it in the morning. It was now late and the daily routine of feeding, bath time and bedtime was started by Mrs Huggett. Later on that evening Mr Huggett was sitting quietly in his favourite armchair gazing into the garden, without particularly focusing on anything.

A stiff breeze was running through the tall flowers at the back of the lawn. He smiled to himself at their antics. They looked, he thought, as though they had all stumbled mistakenly into a barn dance and could not understand the basic moves causing utter chaos to the remaining dancers. Little did he realise that this would be the case with himself when he would in the future actually attend a barn dance. Movement at his feet halted his imagination. Bozwell had noticed that the kitchen door was open and had wandered into the living room. He thought: "This is cosy." Seeing Mr Huggett his tail immediately started to circulate the air, he rushed to form a collapsed heap at his feet.

He curled up, uninvited but welcome, against the slippers, which Mr Huggett was blissfully unaware would in a few days, be spun around the garden locked in Bozwell's jaws or rather what was left of them after they had received 'a good chewing.' However, this was in the future and for the present the scene was tranquil, owner and dog being content to converse without words. Mr Huggett loved this time of day. The girls had finally gone to sleep after the normal two verbal warnings they very rarely needed or received a third. On this occasion, they had managed to outwit him by choosing a new fairy tale for their bedtime story that had gone on rather longer than usual. Zoë had consumed every word from the top bunk. They each had a small piece of cloth from which they were both inseparable at bedtime, moving slowly from one side of their mouth to the other. Michelle, on the lower bunk, did not appear to be paying much attention and was pulling hers back and forward in a bored manner, thinking how she could best use up the two warnings to torment her sister once the light had gone out. Mr Huggett smiled to himself and thought how lucky he was to have the two children, even though when they were awake keeping them occupied was a full-time job. Bozwell at this moment gently licked one of his feet from which his slipper had fallen.

Even though this was not always a sign of affection, rather a natural method of obtaining salt, it could had been interpreted as 'don't forget me, I am part of the family too'.

Mr Huggett reflected that when the family was in full flight and chaos ensued, he sometimes wondered whether the effort of getting through the day was worth the rewards he received. It was at moments like this that he realised they were and in this contented mood he elected that tomorrow he would take Bozwell out for his first walk in the outside world, accompanied by the new lead, unaware that this event would be somewhat different to how he imagined it would be.

CHAPTER 4

Freedom

Michelle lay awake in the bottom bunk, not knowing how best to start her day. The soft murmuring from above her indicated that her sister was not at the moment sharing the same dilemma A quick peep over the top of her bed confirmed that Zoë was still fast asleep, although during the night she had emerged like a butterfly from beneath the clothes and was now spread like a quilt on top of the bed. The comforting cloth still firmly attached to her mouth. Michelle knew it was morning as there was a witness of light peeping out from behind the heavy blanket that her parents had hung over the window in an attempt to persuade their children in Summer that it was bedtime, in Winter the sun had gone to bed before them. A quick glance at the bedroom clock had provided the warning that it was probably not a good idea to start practising her toy trumpet. Michelle could not yet tell the time with a degree of certainty, but knew that when the duck's arm had not yet passed over the mouse's ear, it was not a good time to make a great deal of noise, or leave her bed. She lay there trying to remember the last time she had felt quite so bored. She reflected that it was probably the time when she was a smaller version of herself.

Grown-ups think that just because their children are tiny and do not say a lot, they cannot remember the very early days, but some special children can; such as when she kept throwing things out of her pram, especially the hideous yellow rattle bought for her by her nanny. Passers-by insisted on picking it up and giving it back to her. Time and time again she would wait until her mother was not watching and out it would go, back it would come, until at last she had given up trying to lose the rattle.

She wanted to lose it to avoid people holding it up to her face and shaking it. Even putting on her best smile did not deter them. In fact it often made them worse and they repeated the process, sometimes accompanying it with strange noises which sounded vaguely like "kootchykootchykoo". She did not at the time understand this odd ritual, nor indeed did she now.

She concluded that adults can behave in very strange ways and should not always be taken seriously. Whilst reflecting on the days in her pram, she quite clearly recalled passing the time by chewing her feet, or, to be more exact, the pink booties protecting them. In spite of her best efforts, she found this was no longer possible, which was slightly annoying. She thought how awful it was to be getting older and losing those things, which she could do in the past.

Still hopefully the things she would be able to do when she was older would make up for the things that she could no longer do now. "Time will tell," she sighed to herself.

Downstairs, unbeknown to Michelle, Bozwell was also deciding on how best to spend his day. It had begun well enough as he had managed to wedge himself against the inside of his basket and roll on to his back something he found extremely difficult due to his shape. He studied the ceiling but he had to admit to himself that the view was just as uninteresting as before; still, it was a pleasant change to be on his back and the gentle rolling action also attacked the annoying itch that had been bothering him.

There may have been some silent communication between them as Michelle decided to see if her playmate was awake. She crept down the stairs. Opening the kitchen door triggered off Bozwell's tail to make the customary greeting but, thankfully, not the welcoming bark. After a quick tickle of his tummy, Bozwell bounded expectantly to the door, which lead to the garden, this now being his morning routine.

Michelle could see the opportunity of a game with Bozwell without the need to share him with her sister. She unlocked the door and they both emerged into the early morning sunshine. It was a morning often described as "God given", when one instinctively recognises, but cannot explain why you feel it is good to be alive.

In that one small moment of time, all of nature seems to be perfectly at peace.

The smile of the sun held both girl and dog frozen in a spotlight. Surrounding them were the sounds of the quiet industry of the bees and the calling of the wood pigeons to find out whether any of their friends were awake too. The scene was not disturbed by any loud noises of planes, cars, radios or televisions and the world was in that moment probably as it was originally made.

The scene passed and the picture came alive as the two figures, which, for a second had been still, bounded towards the gate at the bottom of the garden. This was a familiar sight as Bozwell stretched his legs. He had raced towards the bottom of the garden as fast as he could and when reaching the gate always turned rapidly around, pausing only to knock a few heads off the flowers and then he would run like a motor cycle speedway rider around the perimeter of the garden.

Not this morning however. Don't ask me why he did it, I don't know. He probably didn't know either and Michelle's astonished look confirmed that she was certainly not expecting it either. Bozwell jumped right over the gate. A flying Irish Setter! This particular type of dog is not recognised for its deep thinking and it does appear that their brains are for most of the time on automatic. Bozwell flew over the gate and into the adjoining field.

There could have been a big ditch or a pond on the other side as far as he knew and he would not find out until he landed.

Fortunately, on this occasion there was no danger and he made a landing that would have pleased an aircraft pilot.

He sat perfectly still. The vast open space and the fields stretching before him represented unlimited freedom and seemed to hold him invisibly and prevented any further movement.

Overwhelmed for a moment, he sat and blinked. Gradually his nature began to take control. This is the part of you before anybody or anything has had a chance to alter it. Sometimes it is difficult to find out what was you originally and what you have since become.

Bozwell was working all this out the moment he smelt the rabbit. He knew he wanted to chase it, but he didn't want to eat it. Although he had not yet had his breakfast he was not hungry and had no desire to harm the rabbit (he may have thought differently if he had not been fed for several days).

Clearly, there were several versions of himself inside him. The breeze was blowing Bozwell's ears behind him and they fluttered like two flags at half-mast.

This meant that the rabbit was down wind of him; he could smell the rabbit but it could not smell him.

A Setter is designed to set, that is, as a working dog their super sensitive sense of smell would find birds and dislodge them from their hiding place. They should then lie down so that as the birds rise into the air the hunters have a clear shot at them. This was now a rather old fashioned idea, as people nowadays do not need to shoot wild animals to feed themselves. It is easier to go to the supermarket and most sensible people could never dream of killing things for pleasure.

Bozwell's setting skills were therefore largely lost in the mists of time, although his great grandfather may possibly have retained his. Nevertheless, the ability to 'set' had not yet been completely bred out of Bozwell and so off he raced in hot pursuit of the rabbit. The rabbit, still naturally wild, possessed the necessary ability to feel the slightest movement in the ground. It became instantly aware of the charging herd of elephants that were thundering towards it. It didn't need telling that it had better head for home.

His head bobbed up over the young wheat growing in the field and was immediately spotted by Bozwell; the chase was on! If you have ever had the pleasure of seeing an Irish Setter in full flight it is indeed a wonderful tribute to nature's design team. The deep chest powers the front legs, which are perfectly coordinated with the back and the rippling muscles all appear to be working in harmony. A full-grown Setter is deceptively powerful, but even baby Bozwell could still put on a fair turn of speed and although not gaining on the rabbit, was certainly keeping up with him.

Michelle, who in desperation had unbolted the gate in the fence and tried to run after Bozwell, immediately tripped over and grazed her knee. This had only been made possible because her nightdress had ripped at the same instant and her knee now protruded through the cloth, a small tinge of red staining appeared.

In an instant the situation had changed, as it often does, from a friendly game to a dangerous one. She had let the dog out, he was now disappearing into the distance, she was in pain and extremely frightened. The desperate cry of "Bozwell" erupted from her that was a mixture of fear and anger, half choked by the tears that now feathered down her face.

Everyone knows that the winds will always try to help a desperate child and carry their cries back to their parents, even the sometimes-miserable east wind. The warm southerly one which moments before had been playing with Bozwell's ears, picked up Michelle's cry and carried it through Mr and Mrs Huggett's open bedroom window.

A feeling like an electric shock sent them both scrambling out of the bed and they nearly collided as they ran through the bedroom door and down the stairs. Out in the garden their heartbeats returned to something approaching normal as they spotted their daughter standing, looking like a stranded scarecrow in the middle of the field. Bozwell's small energetic figure could also be spotted in the distance.

The priority, thought Mr and Mrs Huggett, was to recapture the two offenders.

The damp feeling experienced by Mr Huggett's feet reminded him that he had forgotten in the rush to put on his slippers. Before attempting to negotiate the beckoning field, he thought he had better put something on his feet. Mrs Huggett had already entered the field and wrapped her baby in her arms and dried Michelle's eyes relieved that she was safe.

The telling off would be saved for later. Mr Huggett had lost sight of Bozwell and so had resorted to calling out his name and trotting in the general direction he had last seen him. After about twenty minutes something told him to stop.

The field immediately at the back of the house was surrounded on two sides by a fence and adjoining orchards and at the ends by a low hedge that Mr Huggett had now reached. He looked out into the distance and could see no sign of Bozwell. Everything was quiet. He carefully looked over the hedge and was astonished at what he saw.

The rabbit was lying flat, apparently unharmed, with its head firmly on the ground. Standing guard over him was Bozwell. His two front legs surrounded the rabbit's head, which he was gently licking. This must have been going on for some time as the rabbit's head was very wet indeed.

If a camera had been able to record the previous events it would have shown the rabbit scrambling under the hedge looking for shelter and Bozwell, with his newfound skill, bounding over the top.

The rabbit emerged on the other side of the hedge to find Bozwell waiting for him and must have initially fainted at the sight of what appeared to be a fox staring at him, only centimetres away and then have been frozen with fright as it waited for the inevitable end of its life. This was not to be, for reasons I have previously explained. Like lots of things, the anticipation of the event, such as waiting for your holiday, is often more enjoyable that the actual holiday itself. Bozwell had had a wonderful time during the chase and was disappointed at his new found playmate's response once he had caught up with it. Initially he tried a loud bark, which should have been the signal to start another game and chase. He didn't even mind if he gave the rabbit a head start in the next race. This did not produce any response.

Bozwell tried nudging the creature with his nose. This did not seem to please the rabbit, but it only resulted in a vast number of fleas deciding that this was a good time to move house and jumped onto Bozwell's head. The only thing left to assume, thought Bozwell, was that the rabbit was not very well. He also decided that a good licking may restore it to health and help to start the game off once again. This is how Mr Huggett found them.

Mr Huggett jumped over the hedge, picked up Bozwell and bundled the dog back to his side. Placing him on the ground he thought now was a good time to try the lead, which he had had the good foresight to bring with him on the hunt. Bozwell's attention was immediately focused on his new situation, which he did not particularly like the look of.

His newfound freedom had been cut short by this strange contraption around his neck. Mr Huggett gently pulled in the direction of the house and Bozwell's response was to anchor his front paws into the earth. There is an expression, which says that there are bound to be problems when an irresistible force meets an immovable object.

Whilst Mr Huggett did not want to hurt Bozwell, this is the moment that all children dread; when parents tell them they are only being cruel to be kind. They know what is best for you and explain that, in spite of your discomfort, it will work out in the end. Whilst all this undoubtedly may sometimes be true, it doesn't really help at the time and so it was with Bozwell who was in great distress.

There then followed half an hour of dragging and resisting by Bozwell to the firm determination of Mr Huggett that his dog would walk on a lead. Bozwell yelped in pain, flung himself over, pulled his head until it nearly fell off but, eventually exhausted, gave up the battle and decided that it may be easier just to trot by his master's side.

He was a sorry looking sight that returned to the house as Bozwell obedient but not conquered, returned once more into the garden. "What a start to the morning!" thought Mr Huggett and he wondered what the remaining pleasures of the day might be. Later that evening Michelle and Zoë went to say goodnight to Bozwell before going to bed. Zoë bent down to pat him on the head. She heard Bozwell say 'what an adventure I had today with your sister' Although Zoë's mum and dad were next door they would have not have heard Bozwell even if they had been standing next to them as only very special children with a very special dog can talk to each other.

Both Michelle and Zoë did not even think it strange. Some things children can do are just not things grown-ups can and they knew this. They said goodnight to Bozwell, told him not to chew his basket anymore as it made daddy cross and they would see him in the morning.

Bozwell thought about it and then decided it was advice he probably would ignore as his teeth still itched.

CHAPTER 5

The Park

Mr. Huggett gently opened one eye, quickly followed by the other and realised that he had been woken early by the usual dawn chorus. Michelle was practising her toy trumpet which Roger, a friend of Mr Huggett, had bought her for Christmas in revenge for Mr Huggett buying his son Russell a drum. Bozwell was barking for his breakfast and Mrs Huggett, in a raised voice, was chastising Zoë for using the milk jug to clean her paintbrushes in. As he jumped out of bed, his brain decided to follow the rest of his body and wake up, duly informing him that it was Saturday morning and he was not, in fact, late for work! Isn't it a lovely feeling when you wake up and realise there's no school today!

It was in this relieved state of mind that he slumped back into bed and started to organise his day. The girls would demand to be taken to the park, which he quite enjoyed doing, and it certainly gave their mum a short rest from their activities. Now that Bozwell had seemed to accept his lead, Mr Huggett decided that he could accompany them and, as the park was surrounded by a two meter high wire fence, he felt that it would be safe to let Bozwell off and allow him the freedom of the park. Mr Huggett had very strong feelings on the rights of animals to their freedom. He always felt sorry for those kept in cages and could imagine how frustrating it must be if they could not exercise as they were born to do. He was also aware, however, of his responsibility to protect animals from themselves as it would be equally unfair for instance to let a tame budgerigar out into the wild. He thought that as long as Bozwell could be kept under control he would not come to any harm and would enjoy the freedom, this time supervised hopefully without the distraction of rabbits!

Having failed so far with the girls, he had also considered whether at some time in the future he'd enrol Bozwell in an obedience training class. The organiser had explained that this was not only for general obedience, but was also to train the dogs to be "shown", where they would be judged and win prizes. As with babies, however, you can never tell how a puppy will look when it grows up. It is extremely difficult to tell which puppies will become show champions; the legs could eventually grow too long or the head is too big, but Mr Huggett was already proud of

Bozwell and knew he was the most handsome Irish Setter in the world, just as he knew his girls were the most beautiful. It was not really terribly important to Mr Huggett for Bozwell to win prizes to prove he was a perfect shape, as he realised he would always love him even if he did grow up to be less than perfect, but, if there had been obedience training classes for children he would not hesitate to enrol the girls!

Mrs Huggett came through the bedroom door with a newspaper in one hand and a cup of tea in the other. Even though she was always up early to keep the household running, she did not object to spoiling her husband at the weekend. The girls came bounding in behind her and demanded their father played the usual game of "'who's the king of the castle'. This entailed them sitting on top of their father's raised knees and being dropped down in a heap at the appropriate moment in the song which was 'get down you dirty rascal!' This silly game was really an excuse to engage in a 'rough and tumble'. The girls concentrated their efforts in trying to pin their father down but were easily defeated by Mr Huggett's insistence that he count their ribs. This effectively reduced them to helpless laughing rag dolls. Mrs Huggett sat on the edge of the bed and wondered whether her girls would ever grow up to become ladies or indeed her husband would stop his childish behaviour. They were all suddenly aware of a rushing sound coming up the stairs. Mrs Huggett, with a start, realised that she had left the kitchen door open and the door from the kitchen to the hall.

The brown bundle shot through the open bedroom door and without hesitation leapt on to the bed to join in the fun. Mr Huggett tried to dive under the covers for protection and the girls howled with laughter as Bozwell's elastic body became entwined with theirs.

Mrs Huggett's frantic efforts to call Bozwell off the bed met without success. This was to be Bozwell's first attempt at art. The early morning shower of rain had enabled him to coat his paws in mud from the flowerbeds in the garden and the pattern of paw prints on the white sheet certainly looked impressive! "Oh no!" thought Mrs. Huggett, "more washing". Eventually Bozwell was persuaded to jump off the bed and was ushered back down to the kitchen. Mr. Huggett decided to quickly drink his tea now and read the paper after breakfast. "Perhaps I could find a tree to climb and read it in peace," he thought.

Michelle had just removed the last of the marmalade from her mouth and managed to deposit it on the edge of the tablecloth, so much easier than using a handkerchief or the paper serviette that had been placed next to her for this purpose.

Her sister had finished her breakfast a few minutes earlier and had leapt from the chair midway through chanting "Please may I leave the table?"

She had to dress her doll for the park – "my work is never done," she thought. It only took Mrs. Huggett an hour to organise the parade. She eventually found Zoë's other Wellington boot, which Bozwell had thoughtfully taken from its normal place in the hall and tossed behind the shed. The prams were lined up; the occupants with fixed smiles looking out from the lovingly hand-knitted patchwork quilts (thank heaven for Nanny!)

Bozwell had looked at the lead with suspicion, but had decided it might be a good idea to allow Mr Huggett to attach it to his collar without sitting down and entering into a tug of war with him. Off they went, the girls in front pushing their prams along the pavement feeling very important and looking forward to arriving at the park. Bozwell tried to walk in a grown up manner, but the pace was just too slow. Walking pace for humans is 'dead stop' to an Irish Setter. The girls too were striding purposefully with their prams. Mr Huggett gently pulled Bozwell back and warned the girls to slow down but, as usual, he realised he was fighting a losing battle and quickened his pace. By the time they reached the park they resembled a cavalry charge. Mr Huggett surveyed the scene. You are probably not aware of it, but parents are constantly looking out for any danger to their children.

Try watching a mother with a toddling child and you will notice that while she is talking to you, the extra pair of eyes that mothers develop never leave the wandering infant. Fathers are not quite so good at this but Mr Huggett still carefully looked around him and decided that the two meter fence should provide adequate protection for his charges. They entered through the gate and the girls parked their prams, laying their babies down who miraculously closed their eyes and went fast asleep. "If only the girls possessed the same ability" thought Mr Huggett. Bozwell just looked, sniffed the air for danger, and sat.

The girls stroked and fussed over him and said to Bozwell "let's have a race."

Bozwell replied 'Do not see why not' and his lead was released. It was as if a starting gun had been fired to mark the beginning of a race.

They all ran towards the far side of the park. Bozwell being aware of his obvious advantage slowed down to enable the girls to catch up. As they ran, not a race for life but just a fun run. They felt the flow of energy between them.

It was difficult to put into words but they all just felt good and belonged together – well, you know just what I mean. As they reached the far side of the park they collapsed into the familiar heap.

Mr Huggett, wishing he was ten years younger but still ten years wiser, followed some distance behind. Bozwell was giving the girls the usual treatment of pinning them down with his paws and attempting to wash their ears.

Mr Huggett restored order and pulled Bozwell off, who looked around to find his next focus of fun and saw it in the form of a small Highland Terrier dog the other side of the fence. The exchange of looks between them appeared to suggest the terrier saying, "I bet you can't" to which Bozwell replied, "Just watch me." From the sitting position, Bozwell's back legs exploded into action and he cleared the perimeter fence with plenty of space to spare, descending on the little dog and his not so little female owner. Mr Huggett cleaned his shoes with his jaw and memories of the little puppy attempting to escape his kennel flooded back. Bozwell tried to play with the little dog

who, like the rabbit, was extremely frightened. The natural response when threatened, although not necessarily the right one is to defend yourself and fight back.

In spite of Bozwell seeming like a giant to the little dog, he attempted to bite Bozwell who in turn was amused at the terrier's arrogance and chased him around the owner's legs. Mr Huggett looked on in dismay as the large lady now became hysterical as she was spun round by the chasing dogs. Bozwell barked furiously and although it seemed to everyone else just a bark, he was shouting to the girls who heard "What a wonderful day" and of course they were screaming with laughter.

Eventually Mr. Huggett arrived at the other side of the fence breathless and in between gasps for air attempted to apologise, not for the last time, for his dog's behaviour.

He eventually calmed the lady down who picked up her still barking dog and marched off complaining bitterly about owners who could not restrain their dogs. "Can't please everybody all the time" pondered Mr Huggett and no real harm was done.

The girls spent some time on the swings, miraculously this time without falling off, and chatted to Bozwell who was now back on the lead tied to the frame of the swing both laughing at what a fabulous day they both had. All three quietly recharged their batteries and eventually found their way home. Both the girls and Bozwell had had a wonderful morning and Mr. Huggett had grown three more grey hairs.

CHAPTER 6

Dollies' Washing Day

Saturday evening was calmer for a change. Some music was playing. The girls knew it was past their bedtime and to ask for the television to be switched on would be to invite their parents to look at the clock. Music had somehow woven a thread into their lives. Was it the soothing sounds they had listened to when safe in their mother's tummy or just the background noise they often heard? In any event, the calming violins dusted the air producing an effect which all the Huggetts appreciated. It was a rare period of calm that inevitably never lasted for long.

Meanwhile Bozwell lay outside looking at the stars. He realised, as probably only animals can, the true meaning of life. As he gazed up at the billions of points of light he realised he could never understand anything. It was all just too big. His world revolved around the Huggett family.

Everything has its place and things move as they should: as does the moon around the earth, the earth around the sun and the bees around the flowers. No matter how big or small the world was, what really mattered to him was the girls and like everybody else, the loved ones in his life.

He felt it would drive him quite mad if he tried to understand anything else so he decided not to bother and rolled over and had a good scratch instead. It was in this comfortable atmosphere that the family retired to bed. Zoë was quite happy in the end to climb into bed as she suddenly realised that it would be a busy day tomorrow because, apart from being Sunday, it was also the dollies' washing day. Sunday morning saw her extremely busy. All her children were lined up at the bottom of the bed and were being studied carefully.

"What have you spilt down your dress Amanda?" she asked and pulled the dress off the doll, throwing it on to the pile of the other clothes that had been removed earlier. Michelle joined in reluctantly. She found it difficult to enter the fantasy world her sister so easily slipped into and often wondered if they were indeed related at all, but anything for a quiet life was the order of the day, so she too removed her dollies' clothes. Zoë was busy asking each of her children what fresh clothes they would like to wear and which dress was suited to which particular bonnet. All very tiring but necessary as any mother knows.

Their parents had always felt that her children's imagination should not be denied and positively encouraged them. They understood that if they could not dream something it could never ever become reality. Life would then become very restrictive, so dollies' washing day required Mrs Huggett to prepare two bowls of water on the kitchen table full of lovely soapy bubbles to splash on to the kitchen floor, providing yet more work for her. Two chairs were subsequently carried into the garden and the clothes were pegged on to the line, which was stretched between them. At times she really wondered if the effort was worth it, but managed to cheerfully accommodate the girls' demands. She was probably the kind of mother every child would dream of having, but to her it was a natural response to the feelings she had for them. Perhaps some people are just natural parents.

The next task was to dress the girls for Sunday school and although Mr and Mrs Huggett were not what you might describe as very religious people, they knew of course that something much bigger and cleverer than them existed; the girls were living proof of this.

As they handed them over to the care of the local vicar's wife, they remembered when they were children hearing the wonderful stories and teachings of Jesus and nothing in their adult life had convinced them not to believe in the message that lay subtly hidden within them. They knew that the girls would have to discover this for themselves as they grew older and although it is true that in order to help them along the path, they encouraged them to attend Sunday school. It helped when making the decision to persuade them to attend to realise that they too would enjoy an hour of peace and quiet! Quite selfish, but they were sure that whichever power was running things they or it would understand.

Bozwell had decided to take a late morning nap. Only the rustle of the Sunday newspapers disturbed the peace and quiet of the Huggett household. Meanwhile, in the church, the children sat in a circle around the vicar's wife who was telling the story from the Old Testament of how God had saved Daniel from the lions' den. Zoë listened intently, her imagination running wild, the images becoming clear in her mind as the lions one by one lay down before Daniel and rolled on their backs for a tickle. Her mind's senses felt the awesome power surrounding Daniel's prison and what he felt when he realised he was to be saved. Whilst Zoë and the majority of the other children were listening quietly, Michelle had been using one ear to listen to the story and the other to hear what the two children next to her were whispering about, a multi-tasking ability she had inherited from her mother.

The look on her face showed that she was also worried about something. She put up her hand and the Sunday school teacher said. "Yes Michelle what is it?"

"Please Miss," replied Michelle, "If God is so powerful why did he let my goldfish die last week?" Not for the first time had the vicar's wife heard such a question and in spite of many discussions with her husband had not really been able to formulate an answer, which could explain this dilemma to the children. Her husband had explained that the development of the world was our responsibility. If we decided to let people in one part starve or die due to lack of medicine, or allow another part to have everything, if we decided to kill each other in war, then this was our choice and God would not interfere.

If our lives were controlled and planned we would be just like puppets. Whilst the vicar's wife accepted this explanation, it was far too difficult to convey this to the children and she gently told Michelle that her goldfish, like all other fish and animals, was part of a natural cycle of life and that everything had a beginning and an end and no doubt this was as God planned it. She accepted this explanation and did not feel sad, as her mum had also explained that following the tragedy, her goldfish had gone to heaven. The vicar's wife continued with the story and then went on to play some games and colour in pictures with the children.

Meanwhile, back at the Huggett household, when Bozwell had woken up he had looked all over the house for the girls and discovered they were missing. He had lay for a short time at Mr. Huggett's feet while he was reading the newspaper, but the sound of the vacuum cleaner signalled to him that it was time to retreat to the garden where he would normally play ball with the children. He did this to keep the girls happy. He realised the girls did not appreciate that he was not, in fact, a retriever who found it natural to collect things and bring them back to their owners. Nevertheless he would chase the ball when the girls threw it and much to their delight brought it back to drop it at their feet. The best time was when they accidentally threw the ball into the flowerbed surrounding what was left of the lawn. This gave Bozwell the opportunity to crash through the flowers and shrubs and use his best gift, smell, to find the ball. After several perfect retrievals he became bored and changed the rules of the game by laying the ball down between his front paws and chewing it.

The girls then had to take it from him. He would wait until they were only a few metres from him, then he would pick it up and remove it to another part of the lawn. Although he could have carried out this manoeuvre all day, he would let the girls take the ball from him after a few attempts.

On this occasion, he wandered around the garden, found the ball, tossed it up in the air, ran after it, but it was not the same without his playmates. So he looked around for some other amusement.

Out of the corner of his eye he saw a bush shimmering in the sunlight, which appeared to be alive with activity. A closer examination revealed that the bush was in fact full of strange winged creatures that moved extremely quickly around the bush. Bozwell, like all animals, was constantly discovering the world around him. He sat perfectly still in front of the bush watching the darting figures and decided to introduce himself. He did this by snapping at one of them and catching it in his mouth.

Bozwell had discovered bees! A small yelp announced that the bee had defended itself in the only way it knew how and had stung Bozwell in the mouth. The bee dropped to the ground unhurt and Bozwell ran back into the house and sat in his basket feeling very sorry for himself and he could not even tell the children what was wrong with him.

He couldn't understand why he was hurt when all he wanted to do was to be kind and play. For the first time in his life he was in pain and he didn't really like it.

Shortly afterwards Mr Huggett was passing the basket and gave Bozwell a friendly pat on the head which brought about not the expected lick on the hand, but a yelp. Bozwell's normally perfectly balanced face was now totally distorted by the swelling caused by the poison administered by the bee. He did indeed look a very sorry sight. The dilemma facing Mr Huggett was that it was clearly a bee sting but whether or not Bozwell had swallowed the bee was unclear. Had he also been stung in his throat in which case the swelling could prevent him from breathing and be extremely dangerous? As with the children, he felt he could not afford as a parent ever to take chances and the vet was summoned on an emergency call. A brief examination, followed by an injection, "just to be on the safe side" put Mr Huggett's mind at rest and the vet's bill made him want to lie down and rest in a dark room! "I should have been a vet," he thought. At least, he mused, Bozwell would have learned his lesson. In the future, the sight of Bozwell indulging in his favourite pastime when left on his own of sitting in front of the same bush and catching bees taught him that Irish Setters do not appear to learn anything much!

At least, he thought, Bozwell must have become immune to bee stings and the bees did not come to any harm, as for some reason Bozwell attempted to roll on them, they eventually dried out in the sun and flew away.

When the girls eventually returned from Sunday school the house was back to normal, with the girls arguing as to which dollies clothes belonged to which of them. "Back to normal" thought Mr Huggett as he folded up the Sunday newspaper and returned to carry out some repairs to the lawn which now resembled a green piece of gorgonzola cheese. The girls announced to their mother that they would like to spend the afternoon painting.

This involved the kitchen being turned into a temporary art gallery, the floor and the table being protected by washable cloths.

Bozwell sat quietly under the table while the red hair on his head was made more colourful by the addition of the bright yellow spots accidentally applied by Michelle's paintbrush. They concentrated on the numbers on the page and dutifully applied the paint in the correct order. Michelle painted twice as fast as Zoë, but the only drawback was that some of the colours were not in the right place and not always within the lines. She looked at her painting and then at Bozwell and thought that he looked much more interesting as the spots of paint had started to run and he looked like a Red Indian with war paint on. When they had finished Mrs Huggett cleaned up the mess. There was almost as much paint on the paper as on Bozwell and the floor, but this was nothing unusual and it was all quickly washed off.

The girls were put in the bath and thoroughly scrubbed. It was early to bed that night, as it was school in the morning. The two angels were presented to their father in their freshly laundered nightdresses, and dispelled any doubts in Mr Huggett's mind as to whether it was all worth the effort raising a family.

As normal he carried them upstairs and went through the usual routine of choosing the bedtime story from the multitude of books on the shelves in the bedroom. They always tried to pick the longest fairy story they could remember. Mr Huggett's aim was to persuade them that the shortest one was the best. He always, however, avoided the story of The Little Match Girl by Hans Christian Anderson, which always made him cry when telling it. As usual, Zoë absorbed every word and became part of the book itself while Michelle chewed the small piece of rag in her mouth wondering what delights school had in store for her in the morning. The story finished, the lights were extinguished, a kiss goodnight and another day had ended.

CHAPTER 7

The Easter Granny

The week passed fairly quietly by Huggett family standards and a broken plate was the only casualty of the week. At least Michelle now knew how difficult it was to spin one at the end of a broom handle; the man on the television had seemed to make it look so easy. The girls had returned from Sunday school and were excited as nanny Peggy was coming to tea. She was a widow as Mrs Huggett's father had unfortunately died when he was quite young. The girls had not known their grandfather as they had only just been born when he had, for some unknown reason, been summoned early to depart this life. Mr Huggett had also been left in some confusion at the sudden departure of his father-in-law, of whom he had been extremely fond.

Although you sometimes have to look very hard, there are often good things that come out of the bad things in life. Out of this tragedy, Mr and Mrs Huggett had learned that when you love someone you should make sure you show them every day because one day will come when they will not be there and you can never make up the lost time.

They had encouraged the girls not to hide their feelings and if sad, to cry, if happy, to laugh and if they felt they wanted comfort and were not feeling secure, not be afraid to ask for a cuddle even though they received plenty of these from their parents; as well as very special ones from nanny Peggy. It is probably difficult to realise that all people, no matter what they look like or where they come from in the world, feel the same inside and it makes life a lot easier for other people to understand you if you can show your feelings.

It was for this reason that nanny was always given two hugs by the girls when she arrived at the house. One for her and an extra one for granddad just in case he was looking.

Peggy was what could be described as a standard issue grandmother. The girls could persuade her to do anything they wanted. She bought them endless clothes for their dolls, the result of many hours either knitting or searching through jumble sales and, much to the consternation of Mr and Mrs Huggett, gave the girls an endless supply of sweets when they were not looking.

Any minor injury would he immediately treated with a tube of ointment always carried by her and the 'baddie cream' was applied liberally on numerous occasions.

The girls could do no wrong. If they were naughty it was all just a misunderstanding. Accidents were only the result of high spirits.

She did, however, look at them in a slightly different light following an incident a few months earlier. For any parents who may be reading this, they should learn the lesson that you have to be extremely careful what you say to children as words not meant to be taken seriously can often lead to unexpected events.

It was Easter Sunday and after church when everyone was in a happy and hopeful mood, the hunt in the garden for the chocolate eggs had begun. Mr Huggett had reluctantly let the children put some paper rabbit ears on his head, paint some whiskers on him and despatch him to the garden to help look for the eggs. Bozwell had watched this play with total disinterest, looking at the large pretend rabbit and wondering who really should be looking after whom?

His nose however, told him that perhaps he should join in the parade. The smell of chocolate was overpowering. Remember, this animal could smell a partridge on the wings of the wind when it was hiding in a cabbage patch! He thought: "gently does it" and slowly trotted up to the kitchen door.

The eggs had been hidden, but they might as well have had two metre flags placed over their positions in the flower borders, as Bozwell knew immediately where they all were hidden with just one sniff of the air.

Mr Huggett told the girls to come and find what the Easter Bunny had left them. Bozwell did not wait for the girls, but dashed into the flowerbed and picked up a box containing a chocolate egg. You can imagine the scene as the family all concentrated their efforts on catching Bozwell and retrieving the egg. Each time he stopped to attempt to rip off the packaging to uncover the egg, one of the family dived at him. He was too fast for them and Peggy, who only had little legs, was soon out of breath.

The girls were now seriously annoyed with Bozwell and the theft of their egg was no longer a laughing matter. They eventually surrounded him and he surrendered the egg with a token growl and all that he had left for his efforts was a torn piece of cardboard hanging from his mouth.

He later said to the girls that it was all very unfair but would they be kind enough later on to give him a piece. The egg hunt was completed, the egg was eaten and, yes, Bozwell was given a tiny piece of chocolate as Mr Huggett had explained that chocolate was not good for animals.

Often all you have to do in life is to ask for something that you really want and quite often you will be surprised that it will be given to you without having to fight or take it without permission.

People can be quite generous if you give them a chance. Mrs Huggett suggested that they all now drive down to the seaside, which was about half an hour from their home.

"Shall we take Bozwell?" she asked her husband.

"Why not?" said Mr. Huggett. The family piled into the car, Peggy sitting in regal splendour in the front seat next to Mr Huggett, with Mrs Huggett separated the girls on the back seat. This was necessary, as sometimes they had hardly pulled off the drive before they started pulling each other's hair. Bozwell sat in the space behind the back seat with his head on Mrs Huggett's shoulder. Peggy talked all the way to the seaside; Mr Huggett had learned that it was not necessary to talk back.

Mrs Huggett was looking forward to the fresh air of the seaside and was drying her shoulder where Bozwell's jaw had been resting.

Bozwell was not a good traveller; his ears had moved back along his head and his brown eyes looked unhappy – and he dribbled! Eventually they arrived at the little seaside resort, parked the car, and set off down their favourite walk.

There was a long wall, which ran alongside the beach to keep the sea out when it was angry and in an aggressive mood. At present it was difficult to imagine that this gentle being who was rhythmically waving at them could turn into a monster which would lash the sea wall with unbridled fury, but I suppose that is the same as people, they can change before your very eyes and have lots of different people inside them. Behind the wall ran a path which they walked along, enjoying the smell and taste of the salt air which was carried on the breeze. There was a fairly steep embankment dropping away from the path and Mrs Huggett was at first concerned that Bozwell, who was now off his lead, would fall down. Mr Huggett laughed to himself as Bozwell ran up and down the slope as if it did not exist, his long deer like legs making him as secure as a mountain goat. The girls had been told to be careful, but Mr and Mrs Huggett knew from experience that one or both of them would, before the end of the day, fall over and graze their knees. They never took them out without a first aid kit.

Michelle, who was the worst offender, had legs which looked as though she had been a professional footballer who had always been unlucky when tackled. Peggy walked alongside Mr and Mrs Huggett carrying on the conversation she had held in the car. The only difference being that the girls were now not listening as they were some ways ahead amusing Bozwell by throwing a stick down the slope to see if he would fall over when retrieving it at high speed. Mr Huggett looked at Peggy. He had learned although not really listening to nod in the right places, although Mrs Huggett was now the focus of her mother's attention.

He had understandably seen quite a lot of his mother-in-law since his wife's father had died and thought things could have been a lot worse if Peggy did not possess such a good sense of humour and continue to enjoy life when she could. He thought quietly that of all the gifts in life that were important the most precious was a sense of humour, especially when things were bad. The world often seemed cruel and unfair, a sort of giant cosmic joke, but even though life was often difficult if you could laugh at it, especially with other people, it somehow never seemed so bad. Peggy possessed this quality and, although she had suffered a bitter blow when her husband died, still laughed whenever possible throughout the day.

She had transferred her surplus love to the girls and with her sense of humour made an ideal playmate for them. They could not, however, appreciate that nanny was older than their mum and dad and sometimes when they were rough, caused Peggy's old bones to creak a bit. As she still told her grandchildren she was 25 years old, Mr and Mrs Huggett did not see fit to interfere with their games and let nanny look after herself. After all, they were only two little girls.

Mr and Mrs Huggett stopped for a while to admire a man on a surfing board play with the sea breeze, which appeared to be enjoying it more than he was, judging by the amount of time he was spending in the water attempting to climb back onto the board. Peggy had walked ahead. Bozwell looked up and decided to run back to his master, remembering that it had been several hours since he had jumped up at him for a stroke and he was due for another one. The girls followed Bozwell like a shadow.

They all grouped some 100 metres from nanny who was still strolling ahead entertaining the wall with a few pearls of wisdom. Zoë was busy stroking Bozwell who was enjoying all the fuss, when she looked at her nanny in the distance and said to her parents: "Nanny looks a bit like an Easter egg".

It is always difficult to tell children they have been rude when you are laughing inside and Mr Huggett did know what Zoë meant as her nanny was rather plump with little legs and could have appeared in a pantomime as Humpty Dumpty.

He did, however, tell Zoë off saying that it was rude to say things about other people's appearance and informing her that most nannies are shaped that way and it was especially useful at Easter when people without eggs play "Roll the nanny down the hill".

His attempt at humour met with a horrified stare from his wife, but the girls responded by chasing after their granny. As they reached her, Mr and Mrs Huggett witnessed what sounded like a stern voice coming from Peggy.

After that she started to run. Mr Huggett had never seen his mother-in-law run before and he was impressed at how fast her little legs were going, but not as fast as the two pairs of little legs chasing her! Bozwell for good measure had joined them.

The Huggetts watched and wondered what was going on. The girls had both placed themselves behind their nanny and were attempting to push her off the path towards the slope. Only her generous width and their limited strength were preventing her from going over the edge and rolling down the hill. Bozwell just barked and was annoyed that he could not join in. Mr Huggett suddenly realised that his little angels had taken what he had said concerning the ancient custom of "nanny rolling" seriously.

He strode after them to give Peggy some assistance in fighting the girls off. What initially appeared as a joke could become serious as she had nearly lost her step and indeed could have become probably the first grandmother that year to have been rolled down the hill at Easter.

Mr Huggett pulled Zoë and Michelle off, Peggy re-arranged her cardigan, which had been stretched in the struggle, and order was restored. He insisted they all walk back to the car in an orderly fashion like a normal family, "whatever that may be," he thought.

The lesson to be learned is that you must always be sure that people understand when you are joking and be careful when playing rough as the cry which has been uttered millions of times by millions of mothers "someone will get hurt" could be you!

CHAPTER 8

The Man in White

Everyone knows that there are sixty seconds in a minute, sixty minutes in an hour and twenty four hours in a day, so why does time change without warning? Why does a boring school lesson last forever and lunch playtime pass in the blink of an eye?

On school days, Mrs Huggett knew that time would put on its best trainers and run as fast it could. In spite of preparing as well as she could on Sunday evening, she always struggled to ensure that the girls arrived at the school gate on time. Recently they seemed to be growing almost as fast as Bozwell and so new school uniforms had been purchased.

Mr Huggett had once again reached deep into his pocket and when buying the clothes thought once again he could say good-bye to his new set of golf clubs. The new school uniforms were hung up ready for the girls to jump into. Mrs Huggett took a good long last look at the new skirts, blouses and jumpers, knowing that within a few days she would be attempting to remove stains that defied even the most modern washing powders. She had long since given up questioning the girls as to how they arrived, the only response from them to the question was always a blank look and a shrug of their shoulders. She had left her husband gently snoring about an hour earlier, had let Bozwell out into the garden and set the table for breakfast. Now it was time to wake the children. Their internal clocks automatically could tell the difference between school days and weekends or holidays. On school days they slept late and had to be forced out of bed, whilst at other times they would wake up at sunrise and start to create a noise as soon as they could: "another mystery that only children know the answer to," thought Mrs Huggett.

They were now old enough to wash and dress themselves with a little help from mum to ensure that the labels did not end up at the front and shoe laces are always difficult. Mr Huggett was familiar with the morning routine and timed his entry into the bathroom after the girls. He knew that they miraculously only took approximate one minute to wash and brush their teeth, which was why their mother always insisted on a supervised bath at night. Mr Huggett had a suspicion however, that when his little girls reached a certain age he would probably have to make an advance appointment to book the bathroom which would, he felt sure, be constantly occupied.

"Still", he thought, "enjoy the blossom while you may, is it less beautiful if it lasts but a day" and he had a leisurely shave and shower before entering the kitchen.

How he looked forward to the cereal with added bran, so much better than the crisp bacon and eggs he enjoyed on Sunday morning.....not! "Oh well, moderation in everything may be boring but it ensures a healthy life," he thought. He wondered as he munched the cardboard breakfast if he would in fact keep to a healthy diet if it was not for the close attention to the family's welfare that Mrs Huggett provided. He glanced down at Bozwell who was enjoying his breakfast of porridge with a separate bowl of milk next to it. It took a few seconds for him to realise that something was different about Bozwell and a broad smile started his day off perfectly when he realised what it was.

Bozwell's ears had been neatly tied with a red bow on top of his head. Over the past few weeks he had seen his wife wash Bozwell's ears after breakfast as they had now grown to a length that ensured they dipped in an out of the porridge as he ate. Mrs Huggett's ingenious invention had solved the problem and eliminated another morning chore, although it had done nothing for Bozwell's dignity; still he didn't seem to mind and he ate eagerly washing the porridge down with the milk.

His tongue seemed to beat the surface of the milk, which went down rapidly, most of it inside Bozwell and only a small amount on the floor. The girls came bounding through the door, Bozwell said good morning by placing a small milky tongue on the new blazers. A sharp "down" from Mr Huggett stopped the greeting and Mrs Huggett quickly wiped the milk deposit off and sat the girls down at the table with her husband.

They were not yet allowed to fill their own breakfast bowls with cereal and certainly not permitted to tackle the milk jug on their own, but were assisted by Mr Huggett who enquired if they were looking forward to going to school, which in fact they were. An anxious glance at the clock told Mrs Huggett she had ten minutes to bundle them out of the front door and start the five-minute walk to school. She wiped their mouths with the handkerchief, which was always kept in the pocket of her apron for just such occasions. Michelle then asked politely if she could have a decorated basket for her dancing exam, which was to be held that morning. Mrs Huggett could not believe her ears and said "You are joking aren't you?" Michelle suddenly realised that perhaps it would have been a good idea if she had told her mother earlier, but she knew that mum was a magician and always had a spare hanky, a plaster for a cut knee or could provide instant meals when she brought her friends home for tea without permission, so she didn't understand what the fuss was about. She watched with interest as her mother sped around the garden collecting what foliage Bozwell had left standing, dashed inside, raided the flowers her husband had kindly bought for her at the weekend and within five minutes had produced a decorated basket. Mr Huggett sat and watched the action in amazement and wondered by what miracle his wife could instinctively change from cook to florist. "What an amazing woman," he thought as he watched her bundle the children out of the door.

They almost ran to the main road over which Mrs Huggett always supervised their crossing. Pressing the button on the lights, she held the girls' hands one on each side. Two children is such a convenient number when it comes to deciding how large a family you want. When the little green man appeared, which Zoë had observed for some weeks and was fascinated to see, he made all the cars stop. Mrs Huggett walked them across the road, kissed them and let them walk the next 100 metres on their own to the school entrance.

Zoë smiled to herself at this moment, as little did her mother know that often, if they were early enough, she would show Michelle just how grown up she was by returning to the crossing, pressing the button, stopping the traffic, crossing over and then repeating the exercise when she reached the other side. It felt really good to have the ability to stop all that traffic with just one small finger. It is strange to think that this was probably her first taste of power, but would be nothing compared to how she would, in years to come, wrap young boys around the same finger.

Mrs Huggett returned to the house, drove the car out of the garage and took her husband to the station. Today was different to the normal routine as he had a meeting in London and did not need to drive himself into the local office where he worked. On the way back from the station, Mrs Huggett noticed that the car was not driving as smoothly as it normally did. She also wondered if the red light on the dashboard that was glowing like a bright sun, had anything to do with it. Deciding that it was best ignored and not noticing that the water temperature gauge was climbing steadily, she pressed on, deep in thought. She eventually arrived home and the car just about made the driveway before stopping without instruction from its driver, steam rising like a fountain from under the bonnet. The tattered remains of the fan belt dropped to the ground.

Mrs Huggett did not give the car a second glance as anything mechanical was her husband's responsibility – she had enough to do. She boiled the kettle and made herself a cup of tea, giving Bozwell a saucer full. This was declared a quiet moment which Bozwell sort of understood and recognised it as a special time when the house was quiet. He was to be good and Mrs Huggett would absorb as much energy as she could before tackling the day's tasks.

As Bozwell lay quietly he could sense the girls at school. It was the same ability that special dogs have which allows them to trot to the front door when their owners are still half an hour from home.

Another of life's little mysteries! In Bozwell's mind he could see the girls standing in an orderly row with their classmates at assembly. They attended an old fashioned type of school which believed in kindly discipline, the teaching of traditional skills such as reading, writing and arithmetic and encouraged a belief in other things that are important in life, like being kind and loving to each other.

The school was modern enough, however, to understand that their Asian pupils would think of their God in a different way from the children who belonged to the Church of England. But love is love in any language so it was an easy transition for the school to introduce as many different methods of worship as there were religions. The assembly hall rang out to the sound of the children singing, this morning a traditional hymn, yesterday it was a calypso gospel.

Both the girls loved music, but Zoë loved it with a passion normally only experienced by lovers with their first kiss. She sang as loud as she could, not to be heard above the others but to add her contribution to the overall sound of the choir, each singer playing a small part in making something much bigger than them.

Being a good team player is sometimes as important as being the first past the finishing line. Michelle sang alongside her sister, not quite with the same passion, she always preferred to have her feet on the ground, but this was an occasion during prayers and singing that she avoided any abstractions.

Mrs Ardwell played the piano with an enthusiasm, which infected all her pupils. The greying hair was firmly clipped into a neat bun. Are Headmistresses taught at teaching college that this is the way they should look? Do they copy their old Headmistresses? Or when they visit the hairdresser do they ask for a Headmistresses' cut and set? Whatever the reason they all seem to look the same. The fingers that struck the ivory (well plastic actually) connected to the hands that represented what she was. A firm handshake to the new children told them they were safe.

A wagging finger warned them to step back into line. A soft stroke brushed away the tears caused by a fall or the pain of a shattered dream. She and her fellow teachers had the responsibility shared only by the parents of the children of helping mould them into what they thought they should be. What a terrible responsibility for them. Suppose the children didn't want to be what their parents and teachers would like them to be? Still it always seems to work out in the end, good teachers and good parents seem to be able to produce good children who grow into caring adults. At the end of assembly, Mrs Ardwell addressed the children and gave them all the school news, also reminding them that this was a new day, which they should use as well as they could, for it would not be repeated.

She announced that several pupils had been selected to be tested for their ability to play musical instruments.

The pre-selection process had consisted of all the pupils filing past the piano and being asked to reproduce with their voice a note struck by Mrs Ardwell on the piano.

Those pupils who appeared to have a sense of tune would be asked if they wished to try playing a musical instrument with a view to learning how to play it properly. Both Zoë and Michelle had been selected and later on that day, after their English lesson they filed in with the other children to a room, which contained several musical instruments, all of which were totally strange to them. The idea was to let the children handle the instruments, consisting of violins, clarinets and trumpets to see if they had any natural 'inbuilt' ability to use them, a modern idea, which Mrs Ardwell did not agree with but something higher authorities were keen to explore. As far as the girls were concerned it did in fact produce a result, Zoë tucked the violin under her chin as it seemed the natural place to put it, took the bow as she had seen people do on the television and stroked the strings. The noise, for it could not be described as music, was not something she enjoyed but was interesting and she continued to experiment. The visiting music teacher observed her with interest.

Michelle had picked up the clarinet and had found that by removing the mouthpiece, rolling up a piece of paper and placing it in the front of the clarinet and blowing really hard, she could blow the ball of paper into the body of her sister. Zoë was given the violin to take home and Michelle was given a note to take home to her parents.

Mrs Huggett had been towed to the school by Bozwell who, although still small, was strong enough to pull a small car, even nanny Peggy would have struggled to pull Bozwell's lead hard enough to stop him completely. This was the first time Mrs Huggett had decided to walk Bozwell down to meet the girls from school and as she stood outside the school gates out of breath, she wondered if it had been the right decision. Bozwell stood, as he had not yet been taught to sit, his tail wagging furiously as he waited for his playmates.

Mrs Huggett was surprised at the attention her dog was receiving from the other parents. A queue was forming of adults and children wanting to stroke him. She looked at Bozwell and realised what a beautiful creature he was becoming.

His red coat gleamed in the afternoon sunlight, his head held proud and the long hair on the back of his legs, which is called feathers for obvious reasons, was beginning to grow. She realised that gradual changes in Bozwell's appearance had gone unnoticed. In busy lives you have to be aware of tiny changes, which are occurring every day to you, or around you, which one day become a significant change. The chain on your bike becomes a tiny bit slacker each day until at just the wrong moment it falls off! It was the same with Bozwell's appearance. When you live every day with something that is beautiful, not only in your eyes but in others as well, you take it for granted and often do not appreciate it until it is taken away and then you notice the gap. Mrs. Huggett decided she would take a good look at Bozwell every day, enjoying the sight. Her other two precious gifts were now emerging with the other children with the grace of runaway trains. Michelle was skipping ahead of the rest and leading the charge. The little tie carefully tucked under the collar of her blouse, the neat pigtails that she wore at the start of the day had been dispensed with at lunchtime and her hair now flowed freely.

One shoelace undone and a small ink smudge on her cheek completed the happy picture of her release from school. Some way behind her Zoë was walking relatively quietly, not just because she was less keen to go home but because the load she was carrying slowed her down. In addition to the satchel carrying her books, which were firmly attached to her back, the violin – although a children's version – appeared to be almost as big as her. The note informing her parents that she had been selected for music lessons was grasped tightly in her free hand. Michelle had unfortunately dropped her note.

Bozwell greeted the girls in his normal way and managed to remove the ink smudge from Michelle's cheek. The party set off for home. Mrs Huggett took charge of the small violin and the girls took charge of Bozwell. Four hands on his lead did not seem to have much effect as they all ended up almost running home in order to keep up with Bozwell's pace. Believe me he was not trying to walk fast, it must have something to do with having four legs instead of two. Do you go twice as fast? They arrived home without incident; the girls changed their school clothes for play clothes. Zoë took the opportunity to dress her favourite doll for bed and while she was doing this explained to her that she would be learning the violin.

Mrs Huggett was not deliberately listening, but overheard Zoë telling her doll Amanda how she had been selected to learn to play. Mrs Huggett could not help feeling a little bit proud and daydreamed that one day she may have a daughter who would become an accomplished musician. Michelle meanwhile was amusing herself by attempting to persuade Bozwell that something really interesting was behind him and he should investigate. It worked really well and she shrieked with laughter as Bozwell spun round chasing his tail. It seemed ages before he realised that the object of his attention was in fact attached to him. He then gave up the chase.

Mrs Huggett did not have to collect her husband from work that day as a colleague had given him a lift home. The change of routine did not fool Bozwell and he stood by the front door waiting for Mr Huggett to appear. The door opened and he was greeted first by Bozwell and then by his wife, the girls bringing up the rear. He always patted the dog and kissed his wife, being extremely careful that he did not muddle this procedure up!

The girls jumped into his arms and he did think to himself that it would not be long before he would have to cuddle them one at a time as they were becoming quite heavy. As he was thinking he may be able to sink into his armchair and watch the news on television before having his tea, Mrs Huggett casually mentioned the red light on the car dashboard and the accompanying cloud of steam that the car had emitted earlier. A brief examination produced the tattered remains of the fan belt, which cools the engine. He fortunately had a spare and emerged from the garage an hour later, covered in oil and not looking too happy as being a car mechanic was not his favourite pastime, but he could not afford to pay the garage to carry out minor repairs.

Tea was eaten, the girls disappeared and Mr Huggett with Bozwell at his feet settled down for a read of the paper. "Peace at last," though Mr Huggett. The sound of Zoë's attempt to play the first notes on her violin as shown earlier by the music teacher, caused Mr Huggett to sit upright.

He wondered for a minute where the noise was coming from. Bozwell uttered a low whine, either meaning he felt he should join in the music making or that the sound was disturbing to his ears.

Mrs Huggett quickly explained the situation to her husband who agreed that Zoë should be encouraged and decided he would buy some ear plugs in the morning. Mrs Huggett had been informed in the note from school that she was to make a small cushion for the violin, which was to be placed between Zoë's chin and the instrument. Of all her skills, needlework and knitting were not top of her list of enjoyable ways of passing the time and often after starting the first three rows of knitting, the cardigan for one of the children would be passed to nanny Peggy for completion. She did however in a few days make the cushion without a fuss and in fact was quite proud of the result.

One afternoon when collecting the girls from school (Mrs Huggett had abandoned being taking there by Bozwell who was now a full half a metre high and strong as a small horse) Zoë emerged from the school without her violin. Mrs Huggett gently enquired as to the reason, suspecting it had probably required repair. Zoë explained that she had politely knocked on Mrs Ardwell's door and, placing the violin on her desk, announced that she would not be continuing with the lessons. Mrs Ardwell, while disappointed, could not help smiling at the way Zoë had made the announcement. She always recognised that it was good for children at any age to make their own decisions and although Zoë had not realised it, she had learned a very valuable lesson in life, which is, that unless you try something, you do not know whether you will be any good at it and it is always better to try and fail, rather than never to try at all; but she had obviously inherited her mum's determined nature.

The following morning was a Saturday and Mr Huggett always took Bozwell for a long walk in the country. They lived very close to open hop fields and it was an opportunity to let Bozwell off the lead and let him run; what a magnificent site a full grown Irish Setter is as it disturbs a rabbit or hare and gives full chase. Bozwell would crash into the rows of hops, disappear for ages and then reappear further down the field.

Once he had got lost and in spite of repeated calling could not be found. Mr Huggett decided to walk back to the house and sure enough Bozwell returned like a homing pigeon some half an hour later. The summer was gradually losing its battle with the next season and soon nature would be exchanging her crown of brightly coloured flowers for the brown leaves of Autumn and on this occasion it had been raining heavily overnight. In spite of the fields being muddy, and knowing that when the walk was over Bozwell would require a complete wash down in the garden to enable him to return to the house, Mr Huggett decided to put his wellington boots on and take Bozwell out as usual.

There was a wide grass path running in between a hop field and a field that had earlier been the proud possession of many golden dancers which had long gone and the farmer had ploughed the area ready for their next season. The rain sat in large puddles between the furrows, but this did not bother a charging Red Setter, in fact he rather enjoyed the experience of the mud splashing over him.

It bothered Mr Huggett more and he imagined he would have to wash Bozwell down with a hosepipe when they returned. What then bothered him even more was the figure dressed in a white Macintosh walking towards him on the path some 600 meters away. What happened next would be imprinted on his memory for a long time. He had been accustomed to the antics of his children and their pet causing some embarrassment, but when Bozwell spotted the man in white he began running towards him. Mr Huggett's heart went in his mouth, his jaw dropped and his brain froze. There was nothing he could do to stop Bozwell giving the man in white his customary greeting of putting his paws on the victim's shoulders and trying to give him a big friendly lick.

The stage was set and as Bozwell approached the man, who had not up until this point in the play realised what that part would be when Bozwell arrived, attempted to push him away.

As white gave way to stripes of brown and the man was clearly losing the battle with Bozwell and from a distance there appeared to be more brown than white. Mr Huggett really thought he could not face the poor man so turned around and went home. This time Bozwell had gone too far and all the hours trying to teach him to not jump up at people had clearly been in vain. It was a dejected Setter owner that returned to explain to his wife what had happened and why their pet was not with him. As expected sometime later a happy Bozwell, who had had so much fun, came trotting back not with his tail between his legs but wagging happily in the breeze arrived home to be washed and dried.

Mr Huggett told the children what had happened, which of course they found hilarious and now over the shock, as no real harm had been done to the man in white, he could see the funny side of it but if you are reading this he is sorry he could not face you and would be quite happy to pay the cleaning bill.

They all sat in the lounge and Zoë was telling them that she had received a card and a small teddy bear from a boy in her class for

Valentine's Day. Mr Huggett looked at his two precious bundles and wondered what new adventures they would have while growing up and remembered a bit of his own childhood and his first encounter with a girl that had inspired him to write his first poem:

He couldn't wait for the paint to dry, too quick the ill-timed kiss,

She responded with a half choked cry.

He'd known her for eternity, first admiring from afar, his love he knew for certainty could take them to the stars.

As he gazed at his love so fair and watched the swelling tears, he longed to cuddle and care and had only done what a man has to do, which surely was not a crime,

He watched her shuffle from shoe to shoe. The pain of being nine!

Mr Huggett thought about his own childhood and reflected that in spite of all the problems of growing up, life is full of fun if you take the time to look for it and in troubled times as long as there is love in your life there is always hope. Meanwhile Bozwell was fast asleep with his legs, which seemed to be growing longer by the day, twitching in his dream state chasing rabbits at high speed unable to overtake them. No doubt he was quite content with his lot, but was unaware that in the near future more adventures were in store with the girls.

They would soon be joined by Custard, a rather naughty cat, who would add to the family stress endured by Mr and Mrs Huggett.

All proceeds from the sale of this book are donated to Challengers, a local charity based in Guildford.

They provide support to disabled children and young people. If you enjoyed the adventures of Bozwell please let your friends and family know on social media. If you have any comments regarding the stories or would like to read more adventures please let me know on social media, further copies available from Amazon.

 @ Etherton_ Philip

Have fun!